Wilhemina Baines

Lays from Legends

And other Poems

Wilhemina Baines

Lays from Legends
And other Poems

ISBN/EAN: 9783337152765

Printed in Europe, USA, Canada, Australia, Japan

Cover: Foto ©Andreas Hilbeck / pixelio.de

More available books at **www.hansebooks.com**

LAYS FROM LEGENDS

AND

OTHER POEMS.

BY

WILHELMINA BAINES.

LONDON:

H. ALLEN AND CO., 13 WATERLOO PLACE,
PALL MALL, S.W.

1885.

LONDON:

PRINTED BY W. H. ALLEN AND CO., 13 WATERLOO PLACE, PALL MALL.

PREFACE.

THE first five of these Poems were suggested
to the writer by stories in a book called
"What an old Myth may Teach," by Leslie
Keith.

CONTENTS

CONTENTS.

CONTENTS.

Miscellaneous Poems—*cont.*

LAYS FROM LEGENDS

LAYS FROM LEGENDS.

ERRATUM.

p. 74, l. 1. *for* A Contract *read* A Contrast.

We see three rocky islands in the bay.
'Twas here of old the Sirens held their sway ;
And still, while gazing on the beauteous scene,
We see the sister group as in a dream,
And fancy that we hear the fatal sound,
Tempt us to linger on the enchanted ground.

. . . .

This is the story that traditions tell.
The Sirens, gifted with a mystic spell
Of fascination, all who sailed along
And heard the echoes of their rapturous song

1

LAYS FROM LEGENDS.

The Sirens.

ALONG the sunny shore the eye must rove,
Till, near Sorrento with its orange grove,
We see three rocky islands in the bay.
'Twas here of old the Sirens held their sway ;
And still, while gazing on the beauteous scene,
We see the sister group as in a dream,
And fancy that we hear the fatal sound,
Tempt us to linger on the enchanted ground.

. . . .

This is the story that traditions tell.
The Sirens, gifted with a mystic spell
Of fascination, all who sailed along
And heard the echoes of their rapturous song

1

Were forced to listen, and forgot to guide
Their vessels into safety, and the tide
Then cast them on the rocks ; and thus they fell,
Unwilling victims to the Sirens' spell.
And travellers, as they wandered on the shore,
Heard the soft strains, and, listening still for more,
Were caught in meshes which they could not see ;
For those who heard could never more be free.
One limit only to the Sirens' sway,
One act alone their fatal power could stay :
The man who first should pass the enchanted isles,
Unmindful of their beauty and their smiles,
And all the fascination of their lay,
Should safely guide his vessel through the bay,
He should be held the victor in the strife,
And with his victory should end their life.

    .   .   .   .

Long reigned the Sirens on their rocky isles,
And dealt out sorrow by deceptive wiles.
Men came and listened, lingered on the wave,
And paid their penance in a watery grave.
At last, Ulysses, who had been of yore
Minerva's pupil in her wisdom's lore,
Sailed on his travels through the beauteous bay.
Forewarned that death would follow on delay,

He deafened all his crew, and thus the song,
By the soft breezes wafted all along
The rippling waves, fell on unheeding ears ;
And he himself, while the frail bark he steers,
Mistrusting his own strength to bear him past
The fatal islands, bids them bind him fast.
Then they approach the spot : the Siren choir
Lift up their voices, and a strong desire
To pause and listen to the rapturous sound
O'ercomes Ulysses ; but his limbs are bound,
And his deaf crew, unheeding him, sail on ;
And so the victory at last is won.
The Sirens, conquered, plunge beneath the wave,
Their voices silenced in a watery grave.

.   .   .   .

The little islets of that southern bay
No longer ring with echoes of their lay ;
No sea-nymphs tempt the traveller as of yore,
And the Campania knows their power no more.
The sound alone the sunny waters make
As the soft wavelets on the islands break.
Ebbing and flowing on the pebbly beach,
Their voices tell us what traditions teach :
That pleasures tempt us, like the Sirens' lay,
To linger on our journey, then to stay

And listen to their sweet seductive wiles,
And bask for ever in their sunny smiles ;
That those who lend a willing ear shall be
Held in their power, and never more be free.
But those whom pleasure cannot lead astray,
Nor tempt to wander from the narrow way
Of duty, like Ulysses, they shall gain
A victory over self, and then shall reign
The spell no longer ; like the song of yore,
It dies in silence and exists no more.

Pandora's Box.

———•◦•———

PROMETHEUS, with his forethought for man-
kind,
Ascended to Olympus; there we find
    He braved the great Jove's ire.
He lit his torch by stealth at Vulcan's flame,
Then back to earth triumphantly he came,
    Bringing the boon of fire.

But Jupiter, from his exalted seat,
Beheld the deed, and, grudging light and heat
    To mortals, he was wroth;
Then summoned Vulcan, and his aid he claimed
(He who as patron of all arts was famed),
    And thus his ire went forth:

He bade him mould a maiden out of clay;
And soon before his eyes the figure lay,
    Finished and perfect there.

Then all the Olympian gods together meet,
The fire-god's last and loveliest work to greet,
  And own that she is fair.

But still inanimate the figure lies;
No sign of waking trembles in her eyes
  Till Vulcan takes her hands.
But at his touch the breath of life she gains;
She rises, and it thrills through all her veins.
  Before the gods she stands.

Then all the Olympian deities combine
With glee to aid in Jupiter's design,
  Their plaything deck with pride;
For known already is her destined fate:
A bridegroom from the race of men must mate
  With this most beauteous bride.

First Venus, queen of beauty and of love,
Herself the fairest one that dwelt above,
  A triple gift must bring;
Bestows more beauty on the lovely face,
And to the graceful form she adds fresh grace,
  And art of flattering.

The Graces robe and deck her with sweet flowers,
And teach her all their fascinating powers ;
    Hermes bestows soft speech ;
Minerva gives her gems, a costly throng ;
Apollo, god of music and of song,
    To her his art must teach.

When each Olympian had his offering given,
Pandora she is called ; the gods of heaven
    Have fitly named her so.
Now Jupiter must give the wedding dower,
Locked in a casket.   Till the marriage hour
    None may its treasure know.

Then on her mission is Pandora sent,
And with her on her journey Hermes went,
    And then the veil he lifts ;
For Epemetheus is the favoured one
To whom th' enchanting heaven-sent bride is come,
    With all her costly gifts.

And gladly he receives his lovely wife ;
No boding shadow dims their future life ;
    Then comes the wedding hour.

Pandora's patience will no longer rest;
They both must take a peep within the chest
          And see the promised dower.

With eager hands the clasps they soon unbound.
But what is this?   A sudden rush of sound;
          And lo! to their despair,
All sorrows, evils, miseries and woes
That every dweller on this poor earth knows
          Have been imprisoned there.

And now, escaping on their sable wings,
For ever will these dark and dreadful things
          Haunt this poor world of ours.
But wait, Pandora; ere you close the chest,
Is there not something else, unlike the rest,
          To charm their evil powers?

Yes; in the fatal box a fair form lies.
Let her go forth; and o'er the world she flies,
          With all those ills to cope.
Then to the tempted ones her way she wends;
The sick, and sad, and sorrowful she tends;
          For this fair form is Hope

Now never more need mortals feel despair,
E'en though of ills they have so large a share,
  For Hope still plays her part ;
And to the suffering she brings relief,
Helps the bereaved ones to bear their grief,
  And cheers the sad at heart.

So runs the legend ; but in our day still
Hope has a nobler mission to fulfil—
  Unlimited her powers ;
For, though dark forms of sorrow, sin, and strife
Must ever haunt us in our mortal life,
  Eternal Hope is ours.

Damon and Pythias.

———◆———

A TYRANT reigned in Syracuse ;
   The people were opprest,
And from incessant wars and strife
   The land could have no rest.

For though he made the city fair
   With noble buildings gay,
He could not win his people's love
   By his despotic sway.

Then rose a few to rid the land—
   Not by an open strife,
But by a secret plot they laid
   To take the tyrant's life.

It failed; and soon the secret spread.
   The king heard what was done.
The plotters were condemned to die,
   And Pythias was one.

Thus spake he: "Grant one boon, O King.
   I do not ask for life;
But that I once again may see
   My home, my child, my wife.

"Grant me the favour that I crave,
   While the short moments fly.
At the appointed time of doom
   I will return to die."

The tyrant mocked at his request.
   "What, let my prisoner go?—
Escape the punishment of crime?—
   Live to repeat it? No."

And Pythias spoke again: "O King,
   I have a dear friend here;
He will be surety in my stead,
   So that thou need'st not fear."

Then Damon, stepping forward, said :
    " Yea ; let him go, and take
My life for his if he should fail :
    I 'll die for his dear sake."

And wonder filled the king's hard heart
    At noble words like these ;
He who had never owned a friend
    Now one true friendship sees.

So Pythias went, and Damon stayed
    A prisoner in his stead.
While the long hours lagged on their course,
    To Pythias they fled.

    .   .   .   .

    .   .   .   .

The time of grace had almost gone,
    The moments nearly run ;
The king was watching with the rest,
    And said, " He will not come."

He who had in his lonely life
    No friend to call his own,

Had lost all faith in others' faith,
  And lived for self alone.

But Damon trembled not, nor shrank
  From death ; for well he knew
(Though he would gladly die for him)
  That Pythias would be true.

.   .   .   .

.   .   .   .

Just as the king had given the word
  For Damon to be bound
And executed in his sight,
  The people standing round,

There came a sound of hurrying feet,
  And there, with panting breath,
Pythias comes, but just in time
  To save his friend from death.

Was ever friendship seen like this?
  It melts the king's hard heart,
And in such brotherhood he asks
  That he may have a part.

He pardons Pythias, and he asks
   (This is the story's end)
That those whose friendship is so true
   Will henceforth call him friend.

The Choice of Hercules.

UPON Bœotian plains Hercules stands,
    Just on the threshold of maturer years,
Between the faults and follies of his youth,
And all the unknown trials manhood brings.
Well-skilled is he in manly sports, and brave
Above all others ; practised in the art
Of wrestling, in the handling of the bow,
In chariot-driving, and in all besides
That makes an athlete. Thus in years he grew
To be the bravest warrior of his day.
But now the time has come when he must choose
Which path to take, and whom his guide shall be.
Thus lingering at the cross-roads (so they tell),
Two women met him. Beautiful are both :
One the impersonation of all grace,
Of dignity, of purity, and truth ;

The other the embodiment of all
That 's most alluring, fascinating, false.
·The first pleads nobly for her cause ; but not
Too highly-coloured is the tale she tells :
For her rewards are not too lightly won,
But after hard-fought battles may be gained.
'Twas thus she spoke : " If you will follow me,
I promise you the love of fellow men.
Your path with roses I can never smooth,
Nor give you days of idleness and ease ;
The gods grant no good thing that is not gained
By labour.   If you follow my behests,
I promise you a conscience free from blame."

.   .   .   .

Then steps the other forward, and she tries
To tempt our hero with seductive wiles
And falsely-coloured promises of hers,
A brighter picture than the other drew.
Thus spake she : " If you follow in my path,
And take me for your friend, your life shall be
One round of pleasure and of all delights ;
The choicest wines, the most delicious viands,
And softest couch shall ever be your own,
Without one hour of trouble or of toil."

.   .   .   .

He wavers, and we tremble for his choice.
But only for a moment does he stand
Irresolute ; then turns from Vice, and takes
Virtue to be his guide through manhood's years.

    .   .   .   .

So may we, in these modern days of ours,
Instil a moral from this ancient myth,
And teach our children that the path of Vice,
Though carpeted with all earth's brightest flowers,
Leads to an end that is not what it seems ;
But Virtue, though her way be strewn with thorns,
Will bring them to the wished-for goal, and there
An easy conscience is the prize they gain.

Zephyrus and Flora.

A LAY OF THE SPRING.

OH, Zephyrus, sweet Zephyrus!
    With Flora hand in hand,
Come visit once again our shores
    And kiss our frozen land,
So that thy fragrant breath may melt
    The snow on hill and dale,
And all the birds in every wood
    With songs thy voice shall hail.

Thy lightest footsteps on the sward
    Leave beauties in thy train,
And at the sunshine of thy smile
        flowers appear again.

They carpet all the woodland glades,
    When, with thy lovely bride,
Thou chasest Winter from the earth,
    And o'er his footprints glide.

Aurora's other sons shall each
    Receive his meed of praise:
Notus with rain-clouds shadowing
    The sun's too scorching rays;
And Eurus, with his lively voice,
    Awakes the sleeping earth;
Then Boreas comes, to shake the world
    With his more boisterous mirth.

But thy soft voice, oh Zephyrus,
    Is welcome to the ear,
For, at thy coming, earth bestows
    Fresh blessings on the year.
Yes, doubly welcome! for we know
    Thou comest not alone,
But Flora, with her crown of flowers,
    Will ever share thy throne.

The Christ-Child.

A CHRISTMAS LEGEND.

ACROSS the snowy mountains,
 And o'er the northern wild,
From unknown lands, at Yuletide,
 There comes an angel child.
He comes (so tells the legend)
 In raiment pure and white,
And round His head a halo
 Reflects a golden light.

Then in the sleeping city,
 And down the quiet street,
Is heard with joy and gladness
 The echo of His feet ;

And all the little children
　　The Christ-child long to see;
They try to banish slumber,
　　But eyes close wearily.

Long e'er the bells are ringing,
　　The Christmas morn to greet,
Each head is on its pillow,
　　The children are asleep.
Then comes the holy Christ-child,
　　Bends o'er each tiny bed,
And whispers words of blessing
　　On every little head.

In dreams the children see Him,
　　His raiment white and fair,
A golden halo shining
　　Around His flowing hair.
And when on Christmas morning
　　They wake from peaceful sleep,
And rise with great rejoicing
　　The Christ-child's fête to keep,

They thank Him for the blessings
　　That He has shed around,

And all the glad surprises
  At Yuletide that abound ;
And pray that He will ever
  Return on Christmas Eve,
And, though they may not see Him,
  A blessing with them leave.

Oh ! happy little children,
  Ne'er may your legend cease
To bring to each at Yuletide
  A dream of hope and peace.
And on the festal morning,
  Amidst your gentle mirth,
For ever thank the Christ-child
  For His most holy birth.

The Angel of the New Year.

A LEGEND.

JUST on the threshold of the coming year,
   With beating hearts, alternate hope and fear
Taking possession of us, there we stand,
As on the borders of some unknown land.
We wonder what there is beyond our gaze:
If the New Year will bring us happy days;
If flowers will spring as in the year that's sped;
Will they be sweet as those that now are dead?
Will the sun shine on us with warmer rays?
Or must we pass through dark and gloomy ways?
And will this New Year bring us joy or woe?
Could we but lift the veil, then should we know
What is awaiting us—sickness or health,
Shadows or sunshine, poverty or wealth.

We may not know ; we cannot lift the veil,
Else would our hearts be faint and spirits fail.

.   .   .   .

.   .   .   .

Just as the clock strikes twelve, the church-bell
    rings,
We hear a sound, a fluttering of wings.
We cross the threshold.   No more fear or doubt ;
The Angel of the New Year stands without,
A Heaven-sent guide, to lead us by the hand
Through all the mysteries of the unknown land.
Then will we enter on the coming year
Steadfast and calm, without one boding fear ;
For, if we follow where the Angel leads,
We shall find grace and strength for all our needs.

———————

LYRICS

LYRICS.

~~~~~~~~~~~

White Roses.

———◆———

ONE' day, as I walked in my garden,
   I saw a white rose-bud there;
Its petals were turned to the sunshine;
   'Twas kissed by the balmy air.
But I feared that the sun might scorch it,
   Might taint its pureness of white;
Lest the dew of the morn should soil it,
   I gathered it ere the night.

But another white rose was blooming—
   A child that was pure and fair;
An angel came into my garden
   And saw my white rose-bud there.

He feared that a breath of dishonour
    Might soil her baptismal white ;
Lest the touch of the world should harm her,
    He carried her home that night.

And I could not resist the angel ;
    'Twas surely in love he came
To gather my rose in her pureness—
    And had I not done the same ?
Then I placed the bud I had gathered
    In the child's pale passive hand,
And I know that my roses are blooming
    For aye in the Flowery Land.

Somewhere or Other.

SOMEWHERE or other she's dwelling;
   I know not the place of her rest.
It may be to northward or southward,
  Or perhaps in the east or the west.
Some day or other I'll find her,
  Then never again will I roam;
Wherever I find her I'll woo her,
  And her land shall be ever my home.

Somewhere or other she's dreaming,
  And building bright castles in air.
It may be that *I* am the loved one
  She is thinking and dreaming of there.
Some day or other I'll meet her;
  Those day-dreams I soon will dispel.
One look in her eyes will reveal all
  I am wishing and longing to tell.

Some time or other I spoke thus,
    When just on the threshold of life.
Since then I have wooed her and won her,
    Now I proudly can call her my wife.
Somewhere or other to southward,
    Where sunshine and flowers abound,
Where sea and where sky are both sapphire,
    Was the home where my true love was found.

The Watcher.

WHEN I launched my ship on the summer sea,
'Twas laden with all that was dear to me;
And swiftly the breezes bore it along,
As the waves made music and broke in song.
But sadly I sighed as it sailed away,
And I stood alone on the shore that day.

For many a day I stood by the sea,
To watch if my ship should sail back to me.
But winter came, with its long, dark night,
To draw its black curtain before the light,
And all I could hear was the breakers' roar,
As they foamed, and surged, and dashed on the shore.

For many a month I stood by the sea
To watch if my ship should sail back to me,

As the waves came in and went out again,
For the tide must ebb and the moon must wane.
But never a sign of a full white sail,
And all I could hear was the sea's sad wail.

For many a year I stood by the sea,
Till at last a message was sent to me.
From over the waters a low, soft voice
Whispered : " Sad watcher, I bid thee rejoice ;
For on a far brighter and safer shore
Thy ship lies at anchor for evermore."

Lingerings.

SEE the golden sun, declining,
  Lingers in the western sky,
As if loth to leave the heavens,
  And to kiss the earth good-bye.

See the tinted leaves of autumn
  Linger on from day to day,
Clinging fondly to the branches
  That have been so long their stay.

See the ocean's tide, receding,
  Lingers to return once more,
And with circling waves embraces
  Tenderly the sandy shore.

So, belovèd, when departing,
  I again my steps retrace,
With fond arms once more to hold you
  In a lingering embrace.

Echoes.

THERE are sounds of joyous voices,
 And echoes of tiny feet,
Two little children are bounding
 Their mother's return to greet.
They throw their soft arms around her,
 And rest their heads on her breast,
As if with each other vieing
 To show which can love her best.

Oh! happy art thou, fond mother,
 To be with thine own again ;
For, though only brief the parting,
 Yet had it been full of pain.
But now thou canst press thy children
 Close to thy heart, and declare

That nothing again shall part thee
   From all that makes life so fair.

But now all is hushed and silent,
   For death's dark shadow is here.
Nothing is heard through the stillness
   But echoes, so sad and drear—
The echoes of children's voices,
   That used to ring through the hall;
Only the echoes are telling
   Where their footsteps used to fall.

Two little graves in the churchyard
   Are lying there side by side;
They are all that the world contains
   Of that mother's joy and pride.
Oh! weep on, thou lonely mother,
   For well may thy sad heart break.
There is nothing left to console thee,
   Save sounds that the echoes wake.

Yet listen, and thou shalt hear it—
   The echo of angels' wings.
Nearer it comes, and still nearer;
   A message to thee it brings.

3 *

And echoes of angel voices—
　Nearer, still nearer, they come.
Thine angel children are singing
　To welcome their mother home.

Waiting.

ALL the spring-time I was waiting,
  Yes, waiting and watching for one
Who I knew one day would join me;
  But not in the spring did she come.
I watched the birds in the branches,
  And as each found his chosen mate,
I asked, Where now is my own love?
  Must I pine in this lonely state?

All the summer I was waiting,
  Yes, waiting and longing to hear
The sound of a coming footstep;
  But in summer it came not near.
I listened to woodland concerts,
  And thought I might there hear a voice.
I knew it would come and whisper,
  And tell me at last to rejoice.

And now 'tis the verge of autumn ;
 Now no longer I watch and wait ;
No longer for footsteps listen ;
 I bewail not my lonely state.
She is more than all my dreaming,
 In the weary time that is past.
It was worth a longer waiting
 For such a reward at the last.

Wise or Foolish.

TAKE my hand in your hand,
 Look into mine eyes;
Tell me, are you foolish,
 Or will you be wise?

For the wise would tell you
 Not to trust your fate
Into my sole keeping,
 But to watch and wait.

Not to put your whole faith
 In the web you weave,
But of doubt or trial
 Just one thread to leave.

They would gravely tell you
 You must *prove* me true.
Will such worldly wisdom
 Do for me and you?

No; we 'll trust love's cargo
  In each other's heart;
Better far to wreck all
  Than keep back a part.

Then will you be foolish—
  Blindly trusting, too?
Yes, I know you love me
  Just as I love you.

Take my hand in your hand,
  Look into mine eyes;
Read there that in loving
  We shall both be wise.

Two Castles.

I BUILT a fairy castle,
  It hovered in the air;
I built it up in Dreamland,
  And Fancy kept it there.
But while I gazed upon it
  A cloud crossed o'er the light;
It overspread my castle,
  And swept it from my sight.

Again I built a castle,
  But this was not in air;
For Love was its foundation,
  And True Love kept it there.
What though the sky o'ershadows,
  And dark clouds flit along,
I fear not for my castle;
  Its rock is firm and strong.

A Passing Cloud.

A LITTLE cloud was rising,
　　Far in the western sky;
I saw it in the distance,
　　And watched it drawing nigh.

Then slowly it came onward,
　　Darkening as it came.
I thought that when it reached me,
　　'Twould break in storms of rain.

I feared 'twould overwhelm me,
　　And deluge in its power
All that my heart held precious
　　In that one dreaded hour.

But when the cloud had gathered,
　　It fell in gentle rain,
Bathing my troubled spirit,
　　Freeing my heart from pain.

And now that it has passed me,
   I only see the light
Shed by its silver lining
   Upon my blinded sight.

I bless the little rain-cloud,
   Far in the eastern sky,
That cleansed my heart from earth love,
   And fixed my hopes on high.

"Yes" or "No."

YES, I know quite well you love me,
   Though I don't know *how* I know,
For, in all these days of wooing,
   You have never told me so ;
And you never, never ask me
   If my heart I will bestow,
So, of course, I cannot answer
   If it's either " Yes " or " No."

Yet I know quite well you love me ;
   I can see it in your eyes ;
I can hear it in your pleadings,
   Though you wait for no replies.
I can feel it in the clasping,
   As my hand you fondly press ;
But you never, never ask me,
   So how can I answer, " Yes " ?

Did you think you 'd kept the secret
   That you never meant to tell ?
Are you just a wee bit angry
   That I found it out so well ?
No ; you never *said* you loved me,
   And 'tis best to leave it so ;
It is better not to ask me,
   For, perhaps, I might say, " No."

A Golden Day-Dream.

IN all my happy day-dreams,
　　When fancy roams at will,
I build a golden palace
　　On every cloudy hill.

I people them with beings
　　Brighter than earth has seen,
And of this fairy kingdom
　　My Love is reigning Queen.

And in the long night-watches,
　　When sleep forsakes mine eyes,
And from my roving fancy
　　My golden day-dream dies,

Still is my heart a palace,
　　And on a golden throne
There reigns my Love for ever,
　　My Queen, and mine alone.

"I Love my Love."

I LOVE my Love in the spring-time,
  When every leaf is new,
When birds build under the hedgerows,
  And daisies spring through the dew.
I love my Love in the summer,
  When forests with songs abound,
And bees are sucking the honey
  From flowers that bloom around.

I love my Love in the autumn,
  When many a leaf is red,
When every sheaf is garnered,
  And all the swallows have fled.
I love my Love in the winter,
  In hoar-frost, and ice, and snow,
When days are sunless and dreary,
  And every leaf must go.

So all through the moon's swift changes,
　　At ebbing and flowing tide,
In budding, in bloom, and decaying,
　　While on through our life we glide ;
Yes, all through the passing seasons
　　The year on its way must wend,
I love my Love through its changes,
　　I 'll love her still to the end.

At Eventide.

OVER the waves of memory I am drifting,
　　Back to the scenes of long past days,
While o'er my childhood's ever-varying brightness
　　Distance shall throw her softening haze.
　　　Yet sweetly the echoes come back to me
　　　Of children's voices ringing with glee,
　　While a sound of weeping, wailing sadness
　　　Comes ever floating o'er the sea.

Only a lost love and a broken promise
　　Can I recall of those past years ;
All else is hidden by the mists of anguish,
　　And by a blinding storm of tears.
　　　But now falls a vision over my sight,
　　　Of happier moments and days more bright.
　　Over the waves of memory floats the promise :
　　　At eventide there shall be light.

Heart's Desires.

COULD I give my wishes freedom,
  They should wing their way
Unto you, my best belovèd,
  And with you should stay.
They should fold their wings, nor flutter
  Back to me again,
Till they brought upon their pinions
  All that I would gain.

First I wish to hear your sweet voice
  Whisper in mine ear
All those words of true devotion
  That I crave to hear.
Then I long to see your dear eyes
  Look into mine own,
Telling me by their expression,
  " I am thine alone."

Oh ! that I could place my cold hands
    Just within your grasp,
So that your soft hands might hold them
    In their own warm clasp.
Could my wishes leave their prison,
    Heart's desires be free,
They should bring my best belovèd
    Back again to me.

Light and Shadow.

WHAT care I if long dark shadows
    Fall before my way,
So that I can scarcely sever
    Darkest night from day !
If the sunbeams from those dear eyes
    Shine across my sight,
I am quite content to borrow
    Their reflected light.

What care I if weeds and thistles
    Grow where I must tread !
If upon my dear one's pathway
    Softest moss be spread,
And if all the world's bright flowers
    Bloom upon her way,
I shall be content to cherish
    Those she throws away.

What care I if bitter waters
   O'er my life should roll,
Even though they break the flood-gates
   Of my inmost soul!
I am happy if soft fountains
   On my loved one play,
And, perhaps, though in the distance,
   I may feel their spray.

What care I if Fate and Fortune
   Frown upon my life,
Tossing me from wave to billow
   On the sea of strife!
I am quite content to suffer
   If my love is blest;
If her life is bright and peaceful
   I can be at rest.

Hearts have Led.

DO not draw your hand away, Love ;
   Let it lie in mine.
Shall we not go hand in hand thus
   Through all future time ?

Do not turn your eyes from mine, Love ;
   Let them, clear as day,
Tell me all the love you bear me
   That no words can say.

Must you turn your face away, Love ?
   Is it wrong to know
All the joy one kiss will bring me
   That your lips bestow ?

You have given me your heart, Love,
   Though your lips are mute ;
And you know when hearts have led, Love,
   All must follow suit.

Clinging.

SEE the ivy firmly clinging
  To the grey and moss-grown tower,
And the white clematis blossoms
  Fondly twine around the bower.

See the woodbine, surely creeping
  Till it reaches to the eaves ;
There 'twill cling, e'en through the winter
  When denuded of its leaves.

Then again we find the sea-weed
  Clinging to the rock-bound shore,
Where the sweeping tide has cast it ;
  There 'twill stay for evermore.

So with rapturous joy I'm clinging
  To the thought that thou art mine.
Where the tide of love has cast me
  Will my heart-strings ever twine.

MISCELLANEOUS POEMS.

MISCELLANEOUS POEMS.

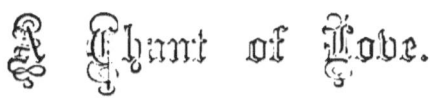 A Chant of Love.

ONLY a year ago, and can it be
    I knew thee not who now art life to me?
No herald did upon my walls encroach,
With trumpet-blast, to presage thy approach.
Why did no zephyr whisper in mine ear,
And tell me that this new great joy was near?
Why did no footprints on the trodden grass
Show me the way my Love again would pass?
Why did no petals of the favoured flowers,
That thou hadst plucked from out the scented
    bowers,
Shed their sweet fragrance 'tween thy home and
    mine,
And lead me from my solitude to thine?

Why did no echo waft thy voice along,
And bid me go to meet thee with a song?
But no; all nature kept the secret well,
And would not thy approaching presence tell.

.   .   .   .

'Twas suddenly, and in a foreign land,
That first thine eyes met mine, and hand touched
   hand.
There had I made my home, so far away,
To cheat the winter of his lawful prey,
And carried to the South a life so frail,
I thought that ere the spring its cords would fail.
(Angel of Death, 'twas thee I thought to greet,
And own that then thy summons had been sweet;
For all my life the melancholy years
Had chased each other through a mist of tears,
And grief, and loss, and sickness, each in turn,
Had bid me their discordant voices learn;
So, hadst thou come and told me to depart
With thee, I would have gone with willing heart.
Thine hand was stayed; beneath serener skies,
In purer air, where fog-damps never rise,
I breathed more freely, and each glorious day
Brought me fresh vigour with the sun's warm ray.)

.   .   .   .

Angel of Love, 'twas thou that cam'st to woo,
And bid me all my fresh springs to renew;
'Twas thou who badst me take again my life,
And cherish it that thou mightst call me wife.
Dost thou remember how I did demur,
And would not let thee from my lips infer
That I consented ?—did not bid thee go,
But answered not thy suit with " Yes " or " No "?
I wavered, not because I doubted thee,
Nor was there any want of faith in me ;
But could I let thee link thy fate with one
Whose sands of life had seemed so nearly run.
My cheek was pallid, and mine eyes had lost
Their brightness ; I had paid the heavy cost
Of painful days, and many a sleepless night,
And thou, in all thy beauty and thy height,
Wouldst stoop to take thee such an one to mate.
No wonder that I answered thee, " Too late ! "

.   .   .   .

Why dost thou love me?   Wilt thou never tell
The reason that thine eyes upon me fell
With so much favour?   It could hardly be
For any beauty thou couldst see in me.
My youthful prettiness had passed away ;
My hair had lost its shimmering, golden ray,

And gained a darker, less attractive hue ;
While tears had dimmed the brightness of the blue
Of my sad eyes ; but still, perhaps, they show
More of the soul within, and thou didst know
Without my telling that thy will was law,
I would not if I could resist thee more.
But didst thou love me for a tone of voice
That harmonized with thine, and fixed thy choice
On me ?   Or was it for the rhymes I string,
And all the metered cadences I sing ?
No, scarcely ; for that fickle friend, my muse,
Did two long years persistently refuse
To aid my pen with her harmonious powers,
And so to wile me through the tedious hours.
But when thou woo'dst me back to life again,
My muse returned, the creatures of my brain,
Revivified ; I thy behest obey,
And speak my thoughts in many a tuneful lay ;
And, as thy love recalled this gift to me,
I dedicate this Chant of Love to thee.

   .   .   .   .

Oh, my Belovèd ! thou dost love me well.
I care not why ; thou needst no reason tell.
Enough for me that I am all thine own,
And I, I live and breathe for thee alone ;

And though I try to pour out all my heart,
'Tis only half—nay, even less, a part—
That I can fashion in this lay of mine;
But still thou knowest all my heart is thine.
I cannot tell thee what it was that woke
The love within me at one magic stroke
Of thy divining-rod : thou canst but know
That all I have most freely I bestow.
And dost thou ask me why I yield the whole
Of all my being into thy control?
I only answer, 'twas the will Divine
That I should take thy heart and give thee mine.

   .   .   .   .

   .   .   .   .

Now that thine own belovèd name I bear,
And on my hand thy golden circlet wear,
I cannot fear that any change will come
To mar the pleasure of this life begun,
This dual life ; I know 'twill never cease,
Not even when our souls shall find release
From earthly trammels ; in a brighter sphere
Each to the other will be still more dear.

Not Yet.

MAY I not lay me down and rest,
   For I am weary, Lord, with toil and strife,
Footsore and bleeding, for the way
   Is rough and thorny on the path of life?
Not yet; for there are others still
   Toiling along the path that thou hast trod,
And thou must lend a helping hand
   To guide them through the brambles and the
     sod.

Wilt Thou not ease me from my load?
   Have I not borne it patiently and well?
Now 'tis too heavy for my strength;
   Ofttimes I fainted from its weight, and fell.
Not yet; for there are others still
   With heavier burdens than thou hadst to bear,
And thou must go to succour them,
   Cheering them with thy tend'rest love and care.

May I not join the one I love,
　Whom Thou hast taken long ago to rest?
And, widowed, I have yearned to go.
　Lord, let us meet in mansions of the blest.
Not yet; for there are other hearts,
　Widowed, and sad, and longing to be free,
And thou must go and soothe their grief—
　Take to them messages of hope from Me.

May I not find the little child,
　The one ewe-lamb I had, so sweet and fair?
Thou in Thy love hast taken her
　To brighter lands. May I not join her there?
Not yet; for there are other lambs
　Wandering from out My flock o'er dreary
　　plain,
And thou must go and search for them,
　Leading their footsteps to My fold again.

Yea, Lord, all this will I perform;
　But tell me, when will these long trials cease—
When may I lay me down to sleep,
　And change this life of toil for rest and peace?

5

Not yet; but some day thou shalt see
  In Heaven a far more perfect work begun.
When I have need of thee I'll call;
  Then only shalt thou hear a voice say "Come."

DECEMBER 19TH, 1884.

———◆———

JUST a year ago to-day, dear,
 I was travelling on, and on,
Farther from this dull, cold England,
 Ever nearer to the sun.

I shall ne'er forget the morning,
 As the sun rose brilliantly,
When I first beheld the beauty
 Of the tideless sapphire sea.

There the pine trees in their grandeur
 Raise their dark green heads on high,
And the soft grey of the olives
 Blend in with the azure sky.

There the purple bouganvillia
  Blooms in beauty rich and rare,
And the bright mimosa clusters
  Shed their perfume on the air.

While the anemones' pink blossoms
  Open to the sun's warm light,
And the red Provençal roses
  Make the hills and valleys bright.

There the misty Esterels circle
  One side of the sunny bay ;
Opposite the rippling waters
  Wash the islands with their spray.

Sheltered from the cold north breezes
  By the Alps, just tipped with snow,
There stands Cannes, in all its beauty ;
  No more favoured spot I know.

Why is it I love that country
  Better than my native land ?
Why is it that I am longing
  Once more on its shore to stand ?

Do I love it for the flowers
    That abound in all their wealth,
Or because its sunshine brought me
    Each day still improving health?

Or because a wealth of kindness
    Beamed on me from friends of old,
And the friendships that I made there
    Brought me happiness untold?

Not alone for these good reasons,
    Not because 'tis passing fair,
But because you " rose your height," dear,
    And you " gave me welcome " there.

Sympathy.

YES, dear; once you told me
  All the sunshine fled
From your life for ever
  With the one that's dead.
Ah, no; do not think it.
  God His angel sends,
To regild our cloud-land
  With the love of friends.

May not my devotion,
  All my tender care,
All the loving friendship
  That for you I bear,
Bring back just *one* sunbeam
  To your clouded day?
It is all I ask for;
  Do not say me nay.

Am I too presumptuous,
    When I wish in part
To fill up the void that
    Death made in your heart?
Yes; I know I cannot
    Take the vacant place,
And I know none other
    Can that one replace.

I have known your sorrow,
    For my trouble came
Just as yours has come, dear,
    And I felt the same.
Still I go on wishing,
    Praying night and day
That my love may bring you
    Just one golden ray.

Mizpah.

" ALL I love goes from me,"
      That is what you said,
And there came upon me,
      Such a fear and dread,
Lest I too should leave you
      (For you love me well).
Shall we two be parted?
      That we cannot tell.

It may be that I must
      Seek a warmer clime,
And so have to leave you
      For a long, long time.
Or, perhaps, some duty
      May call you away
To that northern home, dear,
      Where so long you stay.

But whate'er befalls us,
If we two *must* part,
We are still together,
One in mind and heart,
And no space, no distance,
Can our love divide ;
We shall be in spirit,
Always side by side.

Even when the river,
That for ever flows,
Shall divide our footsteps,
When one stays, one goes;
Still no sad farewell, dear,
Will we ever say,
But just on the morrow,
Meet with glad " Good-day.

A Contract.

THERE are thankless ones who murmur,
　　If a cloud, however small,
Come across their clear blue heaven,
　　And its faintest shadows fall.

There are other hearts that welcome,
　　Just the tiniest little rift,
In the clouds that make a darkness,
　　As across their sky they drift.

There are some who blindly murmur,
　　If *one* pleasure is denied
In a lifetime of enjoyment,
　　As on downy wings they glide.

While some other hearts are thankful,
　　For the smallest blessing sent,
That relieves the gloom and sadness
　　Of the lonely days they spent.

Let us try through all the darkness
   Just to find one little ray,
Soon it spreads across our heaven,
   Turning all our night to day.

And the one joy in our sadness
   Soon will lighten all our woe;
If we thankfully receive it,
   Other joys we, too, shall know.

A Prayer of Faith.

A NATION on its knees, a people joined in
　　prayer,
All sects in one communion gathered there;
Before one Throne with one accord they fall,
And on one Name in unison they call.
What do they ask?　What is the boon they
　　crave?
E'en that the closing portals of the grave
May yet be stayed by that Almighty hand
Whose touch alone can sooth the weeping land.
They ask Him to recall the fleeting breath
Of him who even now is claimed by death.
Will our God work a miracle on earth,
And give to mortal man a second birth?
And can they hope that such will be bestowed
Upon a nation with a heavy load

Of guilt and sin and all unrighteousness ?
Will our God hear, and hearing, will He bless ?
So they may hope, for by His holy will
Even such sinners may approach Him still.
For all dark schism by the Church's light
Shall be concealed, as now all sects unite
In humble faith, and that one prayer alone
Shall rise like incense to the heavenly throne.
The bitter waters of one common grief
Have drowned both anarchy and unbelief.*
Those who disloyal citizens had been,
Now in their sorrow rally round their Queen ;
While those who owned not the Almighty's power,
Fall on their knees to Him in death's dark hour.
Oh, that the country should require a sign
To teach it honour to the Will Divine,
And make it practice, what its boast had been,
Love and obedience to its God and Queen !
And so the people wait, and watch, and pray,
Joining the Church's service day by day.
And they who own a higher ritual form,
Offer the one great sacrifice each morn ;

---

* Just before the Prince of Wales' illness, there had been
a great deal of disloyalty and unbelief.

And those in whom the Roman rule has sway,
In every church atoning masses say.
But still, united is each differing band,
One aspiration now pervades the land,
That God will hear, and spare the Prince's life,
Answer the prayer of people, Queen, and wife.
Not all at once the wished for answer came ;
Still they must weep and call upon His name.
And heavily the dreary days wore on,
Till it would seem that every hope had gone.
But to all those who to the church repair,
There speaks a voice in answer to their prayer
In the appointed Lessons of the eve* ;
They hear in faith the hope of a reprieve.
First, they are told that Hezekiah was saved,
His life prolonged because for life he prayed.
And in the sacred Lesson of the day,
" Is any sick among you, let them pray ;
The prayer of faith shall save the sick," they hear ;
And in this promise they can feel God near.
And so are cheered ; but yet it must be long
E'er night of weeping wakes in morn of song.

---

* Evening Lessons for December 12th, Isaiah xxxviii. and
St. James v.

Not till the dawn of that long-dreaded day,*
Then in His own good time, and His own way,
He sheds His sunbeams on the frozen snow,
And bids the long hard frost and cold wind go.
Thus Nature's God relieves the labouring breath,
By Nature's aid He saves a life from death ;
And in His sunshine and a softened air
He sends His answer to the nation's prayer.
Henceforth, O people! own His sovereign power,
Love and obey your God from that blest hour.

---

* December 14th, the anniversary of the Prince Consort's
death.

Willing Service.

THERE are angels coming, going,
　　Ever, as in days gone by,
When the ladder Jacob dreamed of
　　Reached from this world to the sky.
Now the angels come to gather,
　　All we give with willing heart;
But no gift ascends to heaven
　　That we offer but in part.

It may be a deed of valour
　　If we fight for Christ the King;
Or it may be but a message
　　That to some sad heart we bring.
We may give our costly presents,
　　Gold, and frankincense, and myrrh,
Or a widow's mite accepted,
　　As of old it was from her.

It may be a kind word spoken,
    Or, perhaps, a loving smile
That we take to some dull dwelling,
    And a weary hour beguile.
We may offer patient suffering,
    Or, it may be, anxious care,
For the welfare of our brethren,
    Or a breath of fervent prayer.

We may bring our deep devotion,
    Mind and heart and soul combine
In one act of adoration,
    As we kneel before His shrine.
But whatever gift we offer
    Must be all we can afford ;
For the angels only gather
    Willing service for their Lord.

In the Vineyard.

"COME," said a voice; I heard it,
     And answered to the call;
"Go work thou in My vineyard
   Before the shadows fall;
My servants there are busy,
   Go work amongst them all."

"Yea, Lord," I gladly answered,
   "I long to work for Thee;
The fields are ripe for harvest,
   I labour willingly.
Come, show me in Thy vineyard,
   The work Thou hast for me."

"Thou art too weak and feeble
   To plough and till the land;
The plough-share and the harrow
   Too heavy for thy hand.

So thou against the hedgerow
   Must meekly take thy stand."

Impatiently I answered,
   " Is that all I may do
When there is work in plenty
   And labourers are few ?
If I am weak and feeble,
   Do Thou my strength renew."

Then gently spoke the Master,
   " The hour is waxing late,
Whatever work I give thee
   Is suited to thy state.
And know that those can serve me
   Who only stand and wait."

I followed to the vineyard,
   He bade me stand aside ;
The labourers were toiling,
   The field was vast and wide.
To stand there doing nothing
   Was galling to my pride.

But presently a servant
   Was fainting from the heat,

I bore him from the sunshine
    And gained a shady seat ;
I fetched some cool spring water
    And bathed his hands and feet.

Then, as I watched beside him,
    A little child came by
Who lost his fellow-workers,
    And now, with bitter cry,
He called for them in terror ;
    There came back no reply.

I soothed the poor child's trouble
    And took him by the hand,
I led him through the vineyards,
    O'er rough and stony land,
I found his fellow-workers
    And placed him in their band.

I met another servant,
    Who bore a heavy load,
Its weight had well-nigh crushed him
    As through the heat he strode ;
I took half from his burden
    And helped him on his road.

Then, turning, met the Master :
   He smiled approvingly.
" I did not break my promise,
   I found some work for thee ;
Thou, succouring my servants,
   Hast done it unto Me."

"I Believe in The Communion of Saints."

FAR above the sunset's glory,
　　Far above the sun-lit sky,
Dwell the legions of God's angels
　　Who have conquered gloriously.
Saints and martyrs who have triumphed
　　Through the ages all along,
And our own dear ones who left us
　　And have joined the angel throng.

Though they left us here in sorrow
　　And have entered into rest,
They are ministering spirits
　　To fulfil God's high behest.
When temptation sore assails us,
　　Though unseen by mortal sight,
Still we know they are beside us,
　　Helping us to gain the fight.

In our loneliness and sorrow,
   In our darkest deepest woe,
When no earthly friend is near us,
   We their soothing presence know.
Would this life be worth the living,
   If the earth was never trod
By the unseen soundless footsteps
   Of the white-robed Saints of God ?

When in Holy Church we offer
   That great sacrifice of love,
We can hear our Sanctus echoed
   By the angel choir above.
Let us never cease believing
   That our Church on earth is one.
One in faith and in Communion
   With the Saints whose race is run.

Success.

IN this busy world of workers,
    All must press
Bravely forward towards one object
    Called—Success.

Aiming, striving, toiling, fighting,
    One and all ;
Some may reach the goal they aim at,
    Others fall,

By their stronger, bolder brethren
    Trodden down ;
Or, perhaps, they feel too keenly
    Fortune's frown.

Then, you stronger ones, to others
    Lend a hand ;
Raise them to the higher level
    Where you stand.

They will not impede your footsteps
  T'wards success,
If you aid them in their efforts
  To progress.

And to you who gain a victory,
  Still fight on!
Think not that in one short conflict
  All is won.

Even should you reach the highest
  Point of fame,
And if all the world is ringing
  With your name.

Still be striving onwards, upwards;
  Never rest.
There is always something better
  Than our best.

A Dream.

LISTEN, dear, and I will tell you
    What I saw once in my dreams;
I will tell you all the vision,
    You must find out what it means.

I was standing on the shingles,
    And upon the same rough shore
Kneeling was a pale, pure woman;
    In her arms a child she bore.

I drew nearer, and I listened;
    She was speaking to the child.
While she soothed it in her bosom,
    Thus she spoke in accents mild:

"In the pure baptismal waters
    I have washed thee from thy sins;
Thou art made an heir of Heaven,
    And thy new life now begins.

"I have placed the holy token
    As a sign upon thy brow,
That thou never break the contract
    Thou hast entered into now.

"Thou must cross the noisy billows
    Of this world's most troubled sea;
Only through great tribulation
    Canst thou gain the victory.

"Though the waves may rise like mountains,
    Yet, my child, thou needst not fear.
I will help thee in all dangers;
    I, thy mother, will be near."

Thus she spoke; and then I noticed
    On the sea a wooden raft.
Like the Holy Cross 'twas fashioned;
    This was, then, the chosen craft.

Then she placed the child upon it,
    Kneeling on the crossway beam,
And from thence the woman's figure
    Gently faded from my dream.

So I looked across the waters,
　And I saw a golden light
Shed upon the far-off haven,
　Thus revealing it to sight.

There, upon the shore, an angel
　Stood, with ready out-stretched hand,
To receive the child of sorrow
　In the glorious promised land.

And I watched the fragile vessel,
　With its burden, o'er the wave,
Till at last it reached the haven—
　For the Cross is strong to save.

Then I heard a choir of voices
　Chanting thus with one accord :
" By Thy Holy Cross and Passion,
　Oh deliver us, good Lord ! "

A Vacant Chair.

WHEN Christmas bells are ringing
   Glad tidings o'er the earth,
When children's voices, singing,
   Take up the sound of mirth,
We watch the bright young faces
   Reflect the yule-log's light,
As round the hearth they gather
   On happy Christmas Night.
But in each joyous circle
   We see a vacant chair,
And wonder who is absent
   Who should be seated there.
A mother tells us softly
   (Her voice is low and sad),
" He sails upon the ocean,
   My own brave sailor lad."

Another home we visit ;
　　Here, too, a vacant place.
A look of wistful longing
　　Is on the mother's face.
We ask, " In this bright circle
　　Who is the absent one ? "
The soldier son is missing,
　　On foreign service gone.

Another home we enter,
　　And still an empty chair.
The mother's face is wearing
　　A look of anxious care.
For here it is the daughter
　　Has married, far away ;
The mother's heart is yearning
　　To be with her to-day.

One other home we visit.
　　Here all is bright and gay,
The mother calmly watching
　　Her children at their play.
But there, beside her standing,
　　We see a tiny chair,

And ask, " Where is the baby
    That should be seated there ? "
The mother answers, smiling
    (What cause for tear and moan?),
"The Father saw and loved her ;
    I gave Him back His own."

Talents.

IN a dream I saw five talents,
　　And I wished to grasp them all:
Took up one each day to try it,
　　And at evening let it fall.

First I took the artist's palette,
　　Painted all the livelong day;
But when twilight shades had gathered,
　　All my colours died away.

Then I grasped the sculptor's chisel,
　　And I hew'd a marble head;
But I could not make it lifelike,
　　For the eyes were dim and dead.

Next I sought a poet's fancy,
　　Tried to make a cadence ring;
But it vanished into nothing
　　When I could not make it sing.

Then I took the gift of language,
 And in foreign tongues I spoke,
Till my own voice spoilt the vision,
 And before 'twas dreamed I woke.

Then I wondered what the fifth gift
 That I had not tried could be,
And I thought that in my waking
 It might still be sent to me.

But the spirits of my dreamland
 Were still hov'ring round my head.
They recalled the faded vision,
 Taking up the broken thread.

And I heard a sound of music
 Floating on the silent air ;
Nearer still it came, and nearer,
 Till I met my talent there.

So I took it, and I used it
 To the utmost all day long,
While the morning merged to mid-day,
 And the day to evensong.

7

For I knew that I must use it
    In devotion, and redeem
All those other mis-spent talents
    I had wasted in my dream.

Not alone did I enjoy it;
    Others mingled as I played,
And upon the music's pinions
    All their glad thanksgivings laid.

As I led the choir of voices,
    I could feel the music lift
All our hearts in adoration
    To the Giver of the gift.

Gather up the Sunbeams.

GATHER up the sunbeams
  As they brightly fall
Right across your pathway ;
  You will want them all.
Gather up the moonbeams,
  With their softer ray ;
You will want them also
  Sometimes on your way.

Though *your* life is joyous,
  Other hearts are sad ;
You must try to make them
  Just a little glad.
Some lives are all sunless :
  Only clouds are seen,
And the shadows falling
  Hide the silver sheen.

You may meet such sad hearts,
  Weighted with their woe ;
Then to cheer their darkness
  Let your sunbeams go ;
And the moonbeams also
  In your treasured hoard,
Loosened from their prison,
  Brightly glance abroad.

          :   .   .   .   .   .   .

          .   .   .   .   .   .

          .   .   .   .

Gather up the sunbeams
  Of Divinest Love ;
They are shed around you
  From the realms above.
Those bright rays are precious ;
  Let not *one* be lost.
'Twas the blood of Jesus
  Paid their heavy cost.

Mete them out to others
  Who are dead in sin ;
Show them by those sunbeams
  They may " enter in."

Shed upon their darkness
　Just one heavenly ray ;
'Tis enough to guide them
　To perpetual day.

A Dream of Sunset.

I STOOD at an open window,
   And gazed out over the sea,
With my arms around my darling,
   And oh, how happy were we!

As we watched the golden sunset
   Shedding its glorious ray,
Seeming to linger in cloud-land,
   Where it might no longer stay.

And while I gazed at the heavens,
   They seemed to be opening wide,
While out from celestial glory
   I saw a bright angel glide.

Many were fluttering round her;
   But she left the glorious throng,
And down she came to our window,
   While they sang a joyous song.

I knew she came for my darling ;
   But I could not spare her then.
I closed the window quickly . . .
 . . The angel flew back again.

  .   .   .   .

In the after years of sorrow,
   Of trouble, sickness, and woe,
I stood again at the window,
   As I watched the sunset's glow.

And I mourned for the selfishness
   That had made me keep my love,
In such a world of wretchedness,
   From a home of rest above.

Then again the heavens opened,
   Again the angelic throng
Peopled the hills of my cloud-land,
   And sang their same joyous song.

And one came fluttering earthwards,
   Through all the brightness and glow ;
I knew she came for my darling,
   And gladly I let her go.

I opened the casement wider,   ·
　And lifted my much-loved one ;
On the angel's wings I placed her,
　And gazed till they both were gone.

Gifts.

WHEN the roving fancy
　　Merges into thought,
And the mind produces
　　Poems all unsought,
Think you that the poet
　　Claims them as his own,
Boasting of the wonders
　　That his brain has done?

No; he owns the greatness
　　Of the Master mind,
By Whose condescension,
　　Infinitely kind,
Man may gain the honour
　　Of a poet's fame,
If he use the powers
　　Of a human brain.

When the true-born artist
　　O'er his canvas leans,
Working all his fancy
　　Into living scenes,
Does he take the glory
　　Of his wondrous art,
Which is in his being—
　　Of himself a part?

No ; he thanks his Master,
　　Who all nature made,
Blending every landscape
　　Into light and shade.
He who makes life's pictures
　　Vary with each hour
Gives to every artist
　　Imitative power.

When the real musician
　　Pours out all his soul,
And the far-off echoes
　　Into music roll,
'Tis no earth-born power
　　Which his mind conceives,
But a heavenly influence
　　That his soul receives.

He takes not the praises
  That his talent brings,
But he sends them upward
  On the music's wings,
Asking that fresh echoes
  Of the heavenly choir
May be wafted earthward,
  And his mind inspire.

And the power of loving,
  Just like all the rest,
Is divinely planted
  In each human breast.
We may love intensely,
  If our love be true,
But to purify it
  Is the gift of few.

Some may snap their heart-strings,
  And their voices quell;
Some may love unwisely:
  None can love too well.
We can place no idols
  On an earthly shrine,
If we take our dear ones
  As a gift divine.

Destiny.

STANDING in the peaceful present,
　　With your hand in mine,
I can look with calm composure
　　O'er the scenes of time,
And I wonder that I heeded
　　Both their peace and strife,
When I had not you to influence
　　All my inner life.

Those bright castles that I builded
　　On the shifting sand
Looked so firm, and seemed so lasting,
　　In my fairy-land;
And as each one fell and crumbled,
　　I thought I must die;

But I still survived their downfall,
    And I wondered why.

Now I know 'twas your sweet influence,
    Felt but undefined,
That was ever coming nearer
    To direct my mind.
And, as every fitful fancy
    Faded with the light,
Then a firmer hope within me
    Grew each day more bright.

For I felt that your dear spirit
    (Though I knew you not)
Must one day meet mine, and cast in
    With my own your lot.
Now together as we revel
    In our love supreme,
We can look upon our lost loves
    As a faded dream.

Now we wonder at the blindness
    That could take for gold
All those counterfeits, that tarnished
    Ere their price was told ;

And we bless the past experience,
Giv'n, perhaps, to few,
That has made us rightly value
Love when it is true.

Faithless Hearts.

WE praise Thee for the blessings
   Thou hast shed upon our way,
The dawning gleam of morning
   And the sunlight of the day.
But do we praise and thank Thee,
   When the darkness dims our sight,
When shadows cross our pathway
   Till our day is turned to night?

We praise Thee that Thou gavest
   All the treasures that we prize;
For those we love and cherish
   Do our glad thanksgivings rise.
But do we praise Thee, Father,
   When thou takest back Thine own?
We murmur when Thou claimest
   What was always Thine alone.

We yield Thee not our pleasures,
    And we cannot spare our health;
We keep back just a portion
    When Thou askest for our wealth.
Our hearts are weak and faithless
    If we cannot *see* our way;
We ask Thee not to lead us,
    But we clamour for the day.

Oh! teach Thy children, Father,
    They shall yield and not rebel,
But own e'en in their sorrow,
    That Thou doest all things well;
And teach them still to bless Thee
    Through the darkness of the night,
And guide their faltering footsteps
    To Thy own perpetual light.

Friendship.

D O I hear you say that " friendship "
  Is too poor, too cold a name
For the love we bear each other?
  . . . Once, perhaps, I thought the same.

Let me tell you all I look for
  In the one I call " my friend,"
Then, perhaps, I shall no longer
  Your most tender heart offend.

Well, then, first, my friend must promise
  To be ever firm and true
Never to mistake the motives
  That I have in all I do.

She must be both true and loyal,
  Must not hear a word of blame,
Must not listen to a whisper
  That can taint a friend's fair name.

8

But, withal, I would not have her
    Blind to any fault in me,
I would rather that she noted
    Every failing she can see.

She must lend a hand to help me,
    And must raise me when I fall ;
If dark clouds of doubt surround me,
    She must guide me through them all.

There must be no jealous feeling,
    And no selfishness must come
In between our lives to mar them—
    In *true* friendship there is none.

I must feel that I can trust her,
    Knowing that she will not fail,
But will let me rest upon her
    When no other props avail.

When I 'm sad then she must sorrow,
    When I 'm gay then she must smile,
And with gentle soothing influence
    Weary hours of pain beguile.

This is my idea of friendship
  (Speak not of it slightingly) ;
Such a friend I 'll be to you, dear :
  Will you be the same to me ?

Incurable.

WHERE is thy boasted strength, O heart,
 Where is its power
 In this sad hour ?
Canst thou not play a nobler part ?
Must thou thus fall to earth in tears
 Because thy pain
 Must thus remain
Through all the future of thy years ?
 Arise, and meet thy fate,
 Murmur not at thy state ;
 Work e'er it be too late.
 E'en though that work shall be
 To suffer patiently
 Till death shall set thee free.

A Diary.

DO you wish to read my journal,
 Record of the hopes and fears,
Joys and sorrows, lights and shadows,
 Of the long forgotten years?

No; almost, not *quite* forgotten
 Is the bygone joy and pain.
Let me read it with you, dearest,
 And live through it all again.

I can look at it quite calmly
 While I have your hand in mine,
Though what now seems all so trivial
 Moved me greatly at the time.

Ah! that first page is so hopeful,
 Visions bright of love and fame;
And how often in my rapture
 Did I write my hero's name!

It was but an airy castle,
   That in youth we love to raise,
But how soon it fell to atoms
   You can see—pass on some days.

There you read of disappointment,
   All the dazzling vision flown.
Ah! the tears and lamentations
   At the first grief I had known!

There, you see, I gained some wisdom,
   Thought more calmly, dreamed the less;
And all useless hopes and fancies
   Tried with firmness to repress.

Then a great and high ambition
   Filled my heart and fed my brain,
How I toiled 'gainst opposition,
   Little heeding cold disdain!

I was not all unsuccessful;
   There, you see, I gained the day;
Not alone, Diviner influence
   Came to point me out the way.

And that overshadowing presence
   Never more has left my side.
Do you mark how in all doubtings
   It has been my constant guide?

Then, that page so thickly blotted
   With my tears—pass by that part—
It is but the wild outpouring
   Of an almost broken heart.

Must you read it, that old story,
   Love and faith sought, won, and spurned;
All those letters and these tokens
   Were with this cold note returned.

Yes, it was the hardest trial
   I had known; 'twas better so;
Soon I found both peace and comfort,
   And the wound healed long ago.

Now, dear, turn the leaves more quickly
   Till a brighter vision came.
In the pages of my journal
   For the first time is your name.

Often now, and still more often,
　　Till 'tis written in each line;
Henceforth all *your* thoughts and feelings
　　Must be blended in with mine.

We can shut the book for ever,
　　Now the diary is done;
Surely no more need be written
　　Since your life and mine are one.

Widowed.

———

ONLY one grief in the present,
 One love in the days that are past;
Only one aim in the future,
 One goal to be reached at the last.

Only one loved one to mourn for,
 One name that is honoured and dear;
Only one resting from labour,
 One toiling, and sorrowing here.

Only one motive for action,
 To do just as he would have done,
Striving to finish in her life
 All he in his life had begun.

Only one thought as she labours
 To bear up her fainting heart still,
Trusting to meet him hereafter,
 When she has performed all his will.

Toil, then, through all the long future,
  One knows the sad years thou hast past ;
Only One sees thee in secret,
  And He shall reward thee at last.

The Captive.

IN the four walls of a prison
  Once I heard a captive sigh,
"Is it here that I must linger,
  Live a living death and die?

"I, who toiled in that great vineyard
  Where there's endless work to do,
Work for many tens of thousands,
  But the labourers are few.

"In the heart of this dark city,
  Where scarce any rays of light
Have yet shone upon its dwellings,
  I have toiled from morn till night.

"Through the haunts of sin and sorrow,
  With a hopeful step I trod;
Deeming not my work all fruitless
  If I gained *one* soul for God.

" Now, before I reap the harvest
  Of the seeds that I have sown,
I am bound a helpless captive
  In my prison-house alone."

Then I felt an unseen presence,
  And the prison darker grew.
'Twas the tempter who had entered ;
  Well his evil power I knew.

And he asked in cruel mocking,
  " Art thou thus content to stay
In the walls of this dull prison
  All the noontide of thy day ?

" Thou art doomed alone to linger
  Here in hopeless, helpless pain,
Doing nothing for thy brethren—
  E'en thy prayers are all in vain.

" Wilt thou not rebel and murmur
  At the chastening of the rod,
Fight against the hard injustice
  Of the One you call your God ?"

Then I heard a sound of pinions,
    And the room was filled with light.
At the presence of an Angel,
    That dread tempter took his flight.

And the Angel softly whispered
    To the captive, " Do not fear,
For in love and not in anger
    Has thy Saviour brought thee here.

" He accepts the prayers and labours
    Both of free and captive state,
For they also serve their Master
    Who can only stand and wait."

A Veiled Figure.

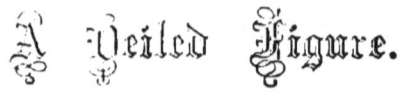

DID you meet a veiléd figure
   Whom you did not know,
When you started on life's journey
   Long, long years ago?

Yes, I met her, I remember,
   But I never knew
Whence she came, nor where she journeyed,
   Nor her name.   Do you?

I could never see her features,
   She was closely veiled ;
Sometimes I would try to lift it,
   But I always failed.

Yet I saw her smile upon me,
   Or I fancied so ;
And I thought she saw some brightness
   That I could not know.

It would make me bold and hopeful,
    And my heart beat high ;
I would try to ask her questions,
    But she passed me by.

Sometimes she would frown upon me,
    As foreboding ill,
Filling me with vague misgivings,
    Though so silent still.

Then I tried again to question,
    But her veil she drew
Still more closely, and more swiftly
    From my side she flew.

Tell me, do you know the figure,
    Have you heard her name;
Do you know where she has journeyed,
    And from whence she came ?

Yes, I know, and you shall also
    Hear her name at last ;
When you met her she was " Future,"
    Now she's called " The Past."

Life's Saddest Moment.

WHAT has been the saddest moment
   That your life has ever known ;
What the densest, darkest shadow
   Over all your sunshine thrown ?

Was it in the hour of parting
   From the one you loved so well,
When to meet again, if ever,
   Neither you nor he could tell ?

Was it when in anxious watching
   By a dear one's couch of pain,
There went forth the cruel verdict
   That your hope was all in vain ?

Or was that a sadder moment,
   By delusive fancy led ;
In your dreams you meet your dear ones,
   Then awoke to find them dead ?

No; I think the saddest moment
  That a lifetime ever knew,
Was when waking from delusion
  To discover one untrue.

Parting is not all unhappy;
  E'en our dead we meet again;
But to find a heart unfaithful
  Leaves a sting of endless pain.

Spring.

WINTER is gone, so let us sweep away
        His snowy skirts, and clear
    The earth of all that's drear,
Waking the Spring to all that's bright and gay.
Spring-time is come, so let the earth rejoice.
        Trees dress themselves in leaves,
        Birds build beneath the eaves,
And join all nature with a gladsome voice.
        Primroses in the glade,
        Violets in leafy shade,
        Daisies beneath the blade;
        Earth, all thy treasures bring,
        Zephyrs thy joy-bells ring,
        Welcome the new-born Spring.

Streamlets, River, and the Ocean.

———◦———

L ET us rest awhile together
   On this mossy rising ground,
Watch the little streamlets flowing,
   Listen to their rippling sound.

See how far apart they ramble,
   Then again are side by side,
Till they lose themselves together
   In the river's stronger tide.

They are just like children's friendships:
   Youthful fancies often rove
Far away, and then, returning,
   Fall into the stream of love.

And the river, is it true love,
   Love that you and I call true;
Does it never break its promise
   And again its vows renew?

9 *

See, it turns and often wanders
   Through those distant grassy glades,
Sometimes sparkling in the sunshine,
   Then 'tis lost in leafy shades.

Well! it may be that some lovers,
   As that river, like to sport
For a while, just in the sunshine
   Of the love that they have sought.

Now, look on the mighty ocean,
   With its sea of boundless space,
Deeper than the mind can fathom,
   Wider than the eye can trace.

That is like true love, I fancy,
   Open, boundless, deep, and free;
For the heart knows not its soundings,
   Nor can faith its limits see.

Quis Separabit ?

"QUIS separabit ? " If the ocean king
    Should his rough waves and storm between
        us fling,
Could he with all his concentrated powers
Sever the cable of such love as ours ?

"Quis separabit ? " If old Father Time
Thinks that, as days and months and years
    decline,
We shall forget, as others have before ;
Tell him that " love is love for evermore."

"Quis separabit ? " If an army came
With swords of slander to attaint our name,
It could not make us each our love recall,
For " trust me not at all, or all in all."

"Quis separabit?"   By no earthly power
Will we be severed for a single hour,
So strong the chain that binds us heart to heart,
No human strength can force its links apart.

"Quis separabit?"   When one *is* bereft,
When one is taken and the other left,
That one shall whisper with the latest breath,
"Love such as ours is shall endure in death."

In my Dreaming.

IN my dreaming thou dost come to me, my darling,
    Thou art folded to my breast;
With my arms around thee as I used to hold thee,
    I am hushing thee to rest.
All thy golden curls are lying on my shoulder
    As they mingle with mine own,
And I heed not, in the rapture of my dreaming,
    That when waking I'm alone.

In my dreaming thou dost come to me, my darling,
    Thy sweet lips are pressed to mine,
I can feel thy gentle breathing as I clasp thee,
    And my pulses beat with thine.
I forget that thou hast gone to join the angels,
    And no moaning do I make,
For I heed not, in the rapture of my dreaming,
    That at morning I must wake.

Yes, awaken to another day of anguish,
    All my pulses standing still,
And beseechingly to Heaven my arms are lifted,
    That no child again will fill;
For I would not let another take thy place, sweet ;
    I shall always love thee best.
In my dreaming thou wilt come to me, my darling,
    Till I waken . . . into rest.

In Memoriam.

CAN it be the sun is shining,
 Can it be the flowers bloom,
While my little one is lying
 In this sad and darkened room ?
All the light in my existence
 Seems for ever to have fled,
Now he lies a waxen image
 On the tiny little bed.

Yes, my mother-heart is breaking
 As I look upon him there,
And for once I feel my spirit
 Cannot soothe itself in prayer.
For no prayer, however fervent,
 Can restore my child to me,

He has passed beyond our knowledge,
  And has gained Eternity.

.   .   .   .

.   .   .   .

As I kneel beside his pillow,
  As I kiss his marble brow,
There are poured upon my spirit
  Calmer thoughts and feelings now.
Even *now* before the cold earth
  Hides my darling from my sight,
There is shed upon my sorrow
  Just one ray of Heaven's light.

And it shows me by its radiance
  That my loss to him is gain;
He has reached the Golden City,
  Free from sorrow, sin, and pain.
There the sun is ever shining,
  There the flowers always bloom,
He is in perpetual brightness,
  Only *I* am in the gloom.

Here he lies, so pure, so sinless,
  With a look of perfect peace,
For no cleansing fires were needed
  E'er he gained his soul's release.

Holy innocents have welcomed
　One more baby in their choir;
He will harp his Saviour's praises,
　And his song will never tire.

No, I will not wish to call him
　Back into this world of tears,
Where his pureness must have tarnished
　Had he lived a few more years.
Though I cannot pray, yet praises
　Will I offer to my God,
Gladly yielding up my darling
　While I meekly kiss the rod.

A Short Life.

GOD sent us a baby
  Just for one short year,
He was, oh! so lovely,
  Such a little dear!
All the children loved him,
  Mother loved him best;
I think Mother loved him
  More than all the rest.
He was like an angel,
  With his soft blue eyes,
Just the blue that's borrowed
  From the summer skies;
And his hair was golden,
  Curling on his brow.
Yes, we all loved Baby,
  And we love him now.

Once a strange thing happened,
　It was nearly night,
Early in the morning,
　Just before 'twas light.
We heard Baby singing,
　Was it in his sleep?
We got up and listened,
　And just took a peep
No, he was not sleeping;
　Nurse said, " Baby 's ill,"
And she told us softly
　To be very still.
Then we heard a flutter
　Like an Angel's wings.
Can it be our Baby's
　Angel voice that sings?
Never song so lovely
　Had we heard before.
Oh ! that we could hear it
　Just one moment more.
Then he stopped and called us
　By our names each one,
As if he was going
　And wished us to come.

But *we* could not follow
　　Where the Angel trod ;
It was only Baby
　　That went up to God.

　·　　·　　·　　·　　·　　·

When we ask our mother
　　Why we had him here
Long enough to love him,
　　Just that one short year ;
Why did God send for him
　　When we loved him so,
Was there not another
　　Baby that could go—
Some poor little baby
　　That had no nice home,
No one here to love it
　　As we loved our own :
Mother says God lent him
　　To us for that year,
So that we might love all
　　Other babies here.
We must soothe their sorrow,
　　We must ease their pain,
Help to bring the sick ones
　　Back to health again.

So that when God calls us
  To our home above,
And we meet our darling
  In the realms of love,
We can say, "Dear Baby,
  'Twas for love of you
That we did to others
  All that we could do."
So that little lifetime,
  Though it was so short,
Was not all unfruitful,
  Was not lived for nought.

· · · · · ·

This is Mother's answer,
  And she must know best,
For she loves our Baby
  More than all the rest.

LONDON:
PRINTED BY W. H. ALLEN AND CO., 13 WATERLOO PLACE, S.W.

www.ingramcontent.com/pod-product-compliance
Lightning Source LLC
Chambersburg PA
CBHW021124020726
47500CB00003B/914